The Swiss Family Robinson

JOHANN WYSS

Level 3

Retold by Madeleine du Vivier
Series Editors: Andy Hopkins and Jocelyn Potter

T0346363

Pearson Education Limited
Edinburgh Gate, Harlow,
Essex CM20 2JE, England
and Associated Companies throughout the world.

ISBN: 978-1-4058-5548-8

First published by Penguin Books 2000
This edition published 2008

15

Text copyright © Penguin Books Ltd 2000
This edition copyright © Pearson Education Ltd 2008
Illustrations by Mark Peppé
Opening illustration by Alan Fraser

Typeset by Graphicraft Ltd, Hong Kong
Set in 11/14pt Bembo
Printed in China
SWTC/15

Published by Pearson Education Ltd

Every effort has been made to trace the copyright holders and we apologise in advance
for any unintentional omissions. We would be pleased to insert the appropriate
acknowledgement in any subsequent edition of this publication.

For a complete list of the titles available in the Pearson English Readers series, please visit
www.pearsonenglishreaders.com. Alternatively, write to your local Pearson Education
office or to Pearson English Readers Marketing Department, Pearson Education,
Edinburgh Gate, Harlow, Essex CM20 2JE, England.

Contents

Introduction

It was the seventh day of the storm. We didn't know where we were. Everyone on the ship believed that death was very near. My wife and my four young sons moved close to me.

'My dear children,' I said, 'I don't think we're going to die.'

Then, above the noise of the storm, I heard a cry: 'Land! Land!' And the ship hit the rocks.

The family do not die at sea; they find their way to a small island. But what can they do now? Where will they live? What will they eat? Luckily, the father and mother have useful skills and they can teach their children. But how long will they be there, on the island?

The writer of this story, Johann Rudolph Wyss (1782–1830), was a teacher at a university in Berne, in Switzerland. He was very interested in the stories that parents have told to their children for hundreds of years. But Wyss is remembered by most people because, in 1812, he wrote *The Swiss Family Robinson*.

Wyss took the idea for *The Swiss Family Robinson* from another famous story, *Robinson Crusoe* by Daniel Defoe. Defoe wrote his book after he heard about the real adventures of Alexander Selkirk. Selkirk had a fight with an officer on his ship, and in 1704 he was left on the island of Juan Fernandez. Later, Selkirk was taken off the island by another ship, but he spent years alone there.

Daniel Defoe took Alexander Selkirk's story and added to it. *Robinson Crusoe* (1719) was not a true story. But many people believed that it was. At that time there were not many books that told a story. The descriptions in the book seemed very real. Robinson Crusoe uses things that he brings from his ship. He also uses things that he finds on the island. He grows plants to eat. He builds a house and makes a canoe. He tries not to go crazy during his long years alone on the island. And then he finds that he is not alone . . .

The Swiss Family Robinson is different in a number of ways, but one difference is very important. *Robinson Crusoe* was not written to teach any special lessons. *The Swiss Family Robinson* shows that a loving family can work together in very difficult times. The story is told by the father. He teaches his sons lessons that readers of the book can also learn. The children have to learn to be kind and patient. They have to work hard and help their parents and their brothers. They are alone, but together, and they must always think of other people. No one ever gets angry or shouts on the island. Perhaps people in those days showed their feelings less and thought about themselves less than people today.

Wyss's book is very long – he wrote it as two books – and the father often talks about religion to his sons. This shorter book tells the more exciting and adventurous parts of the story as we watch the boys grow up in their island home.

Wyss didn't finish the story. A lot of people added bits to it over the years, until it reached its final form in English in about 1889. Wyss's story had no real ending. Later writers added the English girl Jenny, and the return of Jenny and Fritz to England. Other people then came to the island and they started a new country called 'New Switzerland'.

At the time of the story, ships often carried birds and animals. Some of these were owned by passengers who were on their way to new lives in other countries. Some of the animals were there as fresh food on long sea trips. The sailing ships were slow in those days, and there were no tins of food or fridges.

Passengers on these long sea trips to new countries were often very good with their hands. They could build houses and make gardens, so the skills of the father and mother in Wyss's story were not unusual.

The Swiss family were very lucky to find so many animals, plants and other useful things on one small island. This was not surprising for the first readers of the book, because they did not know much about many parts of the world. Wyss probably read about James Cook's journeys to the South Pacific, between 1768 and 1779. But there was still a lot that people did not know about those islands.

These days, it is more difficult to believe in the island, but *The Swiss Family Robinson* is still an interesting and exciting story for people of all ages. It shows that with strong minds and useful skills, people can build their lives again in a new, strange place.

Today there are few unknown places left in the world, but the Robinson Crusoe idea still excites people's imaginations. The film *Cast Away* (2000), starring Tom Hanks, tells the story of a man who lives through an air crash. He is thought to be dead, so nobody looks for him. He lives on a rocky island in the Pacific for years. He draws a face on a ball and talks to it, and that is his only friend. In the popular television show *Lost*, forty-eight people find themselves on a Pacific island when their aeroplane from Sydney crashes there. But these are people from the modern world, and they do not live their lives like the Swiss Family Robinson.

Some of the Animals in this Story

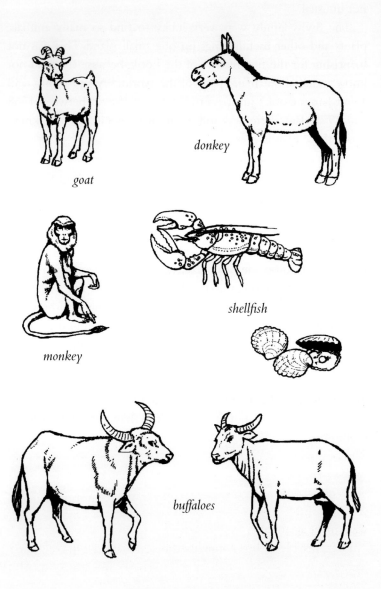

goat

donkey

monkey

shellfish

buffaloes

Chapter 1   Ship on the Rocks

It was the seventh day of the storm. We didn't know where we were. Everyone on the ship believed that death was very near. My wife and my four young sons moved close to me.

'My dear children,' I said, 'I don't think we're going to die.'

Then, above the noise of the storm, I heard a cry: 'Land! Land!' And the ship hit the rocks.

We heard someone shout, 'There's no hope now. Let down the boats.'

'No hope!' cried the children.

'Be brave, my boys,' I said. 'The land isn't far away. We'll save ourselves – we'll find a way. I'll see what we can do.'

I left our room and looked around, but there were no sailors on the ship. They were all in boats on the sea. We were alone!

I returned to my family. 'It's all right,' I said. 'The front part of the ship is between two rocks, so it's above the water. Tomorrow the sea will be calmer and we'll be able to reach the land.'

The children immediately became happier, but my wife understood the danger of our position. She prepared a meal and the boys went to bed, but my wife and I stayed awake and watched.

◆

The next day, it was not as windy and the sky was clear. We could see that we were near land.

'Now,' I said, 'let's go round the ship. Let's look for things that will help us to reach the land. We need food and water too. Then we'll meet again here.'

Fritz, my oldest boy, brought back guns and gunpowder. My second son, Ernest, found a box of tools, a lot of nails, a big knife, some small knives and some other things. The box was very heavy, but Fritz helped him with it.

When my third son, Jack, opened the door to one of the rooms, two big dogs jumped out at him. They were quite friendly and he brought them with him.

Then my wife came with Franz, our youngest son.

'Good news,' she said. 'A donkey, two goats, a pig, six sheep and some chickens are still alive.'

I said, 'Those will all be useful – but not the dogs. They'll eat too much.'

'But Father,' said Jack, 'they'll help us to catch animals for food when we reach the land.'

'Yes,' I said, 'but we haven't reached it yet. We need to make a boat. Let's get some barrels and some pieces of wood.'

So we started to work and we made a boat. We used one of the pieces of wood to hold the sail.

At last everything was ready, and we lowered the boat into the sea. It was too late to leave the ship that night so I tied one end of a long rope to our boat and the other end to the ship. Then we had a meal and went to bed.

Chapter 2   The Island

We all woke up early the next morning. I called the children together and said, 'First, we must feed the animals. I hope we'll be able to come back for them later. Then let's take everything that will be useful to us.'

We took guns and gunpowder, and bags of food. We took some cooking pots, the tools, nails and knives. We brought sailcloth to make a tent. The chickens seemed sad, so we brought them too.

'The dogs,' I said, 'can swim behind the boat.'

At the last minute my wife came, carrying a big bag. I didn't ask her what was in it.

At first, the boat turned round and round, but after a time I learned to sail it.

'Look!' cried Fritz, as we came nearer the land. 'Those are coconuts. We'll have coconuts to eat.'

The dogs were swimming towards calmer water.

'They know the best place to land,' I said. 'I'll follow them.'

Three of the boys jumped on to the beach. Then they helped Franz to follow them. We took everything out of the boat and freed the chickens. Then I cut some wood from the trees, put it in the ground and made a tent from the sailcloth.

'Now,' I said to the children, 'go and bring some dry grass for our beds.'

While they were doing this, I found some big stones for a fireplace. I soon made a good fire, using dry wood from the beach. My wife got a pot of water from the river and put it on the fire. Then, helped by little Franz, she began to cook a meal.

Fritz took a gun to the other side of the river. Ernest went to the right along the beach and Jack went to the left. Suddenly, I heard Jack shouting. I took a gun and ran to help him. I found him standing in water up to his knees.

'Come here, Father,' he shouted. 'Come quickly. I've caught something really big!'

'All right,' I said, 'bring it here.'

'I can't. It's caught me.'

I laughed. Then I hit the large shellfish with my gun and freed Jack. It was only holding on to his clothing, so he wasn't hurt.

'Well, Jack,' I said, 'you've caught our first fresh food.'

Just then, Ernest came. 'I've found some things that are good to eat too. But I need help to get them.'

'What are they?'

'They're shellfish too, but I can't get them off the rocks. We'll take them later, after our meal.'

'The food's ready,' said my wife, 'but we should wait for Fritz.'

She looked at her pot. 'How shall we eat it? We can't eat soup with a knife! We need spoons, but we haven't got any!'

'We can cut coconuts in half and use them.'

'We can, but we haven't got any coconuts,' I said.

'There are the shells on the rocks!' said Ernest. 'We can use them if you help me.'

Fritz arrived, so the boys all went to get the shellfish. When they came back, Jack tried to open one with a knife.

'I can't do it!' he said. 'I can't open it.'

'Put them near the hot fire,' I said, 'and they'll open without your help.'

So we sat down to our meal. We ate the shellfish first, and then we used the shells as spoons for the soup.

'But we haven't got any plates!' said my wife.

'I've got a plate,' said Ernest, showing her a very big shell. 'I found it on the beach. There are lots of these shells near the place where I found this one.'

'Then why,' I asked, 'didn't you bring plates for all of us?'

The sun was going down when we finished our meal. Then my wife opened her bag from the ship and began to throw corn to the chickens. I stopped her.

'I'm very glad that you've brought this. But we mustn't give it to the chickens. We must plant it. Then, when it grows, we can make bread. The chickens can have other food.'

It was time for everyone to go to bed. We took our guns with us into the tent.

Chapter 3   The Baby Monkey

We woke up very early the next day.

'First,' I said, 'we must see if any of the sailors from the ship have reached land.'

'We don't all need to go,' said my wife. 'You take Fritz. I'll stay here with the other boys.'

'Yes,' I answered, 'I'll take Turk with us, and Flora can stay with you.' Those were the names of our dogs.

My wife gave us bags of food to take with us. We walked along the beach, looking in the sand for signs of other people. But we didn't find any.

Fritz had a gun with him. 'Shall I use the gun?' he asked. 'If they're near, they'll hear it.'

'No!' I said. 'If there are wild men on the island, they will hear it too. We don't want them to know we're here.'

We turned away from the beach and walked for about a mile. We came to a little wood. At every step, we saw a new and beautiful plant.

'What's this strange plant,' asked Fritz, 'with these big things growing on it?'

'Ah,' I said, 'those are gourds. They're very useful.'

We took some of the gourds and cut them open.

'Now we must take out the soft part, inside. We'll leave the shells to dry in the sun. Then we can make spoons and plates and cooking pots from them. That's why these plants are so useful.'

'I don't understand how you can make a cooking pot from this. If you put it on the fire, it'll burn.'

'Ah,' I said, 'but you don't put it on the fire. You fill it with water. Then you put hot stones into the water, and the water will boil.'

We cut plates and spoons and pots from the gourds, and put them in the sun. We left signs to ourselves around the place, so we could find it again later.

We walked to a field of very tall grass. It was growing high above our heads.

'Now where,' I thought, 'have I seen grass like this?'

We had to cut our way through the grass. As I touched it, my hands became very wet. I put a hand to my mouth – then I remembered!

'Come here, Fritz. Cut one of these open and put the soft part in your mouth.'

He did that. 'Oh!' he said. 'It's sweet. Like sugar!'

'It *is* sugar,' I answered. 'Let's take some back with us. The others will be very pleased and surprised.'

Next, we came to some coconut trees. As we moved nearer, we saw a lot of monkeys on the ground near the trees. But when they saw us, they ran up into the trees. They made angry noises at us. Fritz lifted his gun.

'Stop!' I cried. 'Why do you want to kill those monkeys?'

'Because they're screaming at us. They're terrible, useless things.'

'Or perhaps they're laughing at you. Why are you getting so angry because they're laughing at you? They're right to laugh at an angry boy. And they aren't useless.'

'How can you make a monkey useful?' Fritz asked.

I threw some stones at the monkeys in the trees, and the monkeys threw coconuts down at us.

'There!' I said. 'An angry monkey can be quite useful.'

'More useful than an angry boy?' said Fritz. 'But I'm not angry now. I'll carry the coconuts.'

We came to more coconut trees, and the dog, Turk, ran in front of us. We heard cries of pain, and angry cries from the monkeys up in the trees. We saw that Turk had one of the monkeys in his mouth.

Fritz ran to save it. But it was too late – the monkey was dead. Its baby wasn't far away. It was in the grass, crying out in fear. Then a very strange thing happened. The baby monkey jumped on to Fritz's back and held on to his hair.

'Take it off! Take it off!' cried Fritz.

I laughed. 'It's lost its mother, and so you've become its father. Yes, it's very similar to its new father!'

. . . the monkeys threw coconuts down at us.

I carefully took the monkey off Fritz's back and held it in my arms.

'What shall we do with it?' I asked.

'Can I take it home?' cried Fritz. 'I'll get milk for it from the goats on the ship, and soon it will learn to find food for itself.'

◆

We returned to the beach, and my wife and the three other boys ran to meet us. They were very pleased to see the little monkey.

'What are those sticks?' they asked.

'They're for you to eat,' said Fritz, and he gave the sugar to his brothers.

A very good meal was waiting for us at the tent. Different sorts of fish and a bird were cooking over the fire. Franz caught the fish while we were away. Ernest caught the bird. The fish was very nice, but we didn't like the taste of Ernest's bird.

The sun was going down when we finished our meal. We all went to bed – Fritz took the little monkey with him.

Chapter 4   Back to the Ship

When I woke up, I said to my wife, 'I don't know what to do first. There are so many things that we need to do.'

'First,' she said, 'you must bring those animals from the ship. Go with Fritz. The rest of us will look for a place where we can build a home.'

I said to her, 'We'll have to stay on the ship all night. Tell Ernest to climb up that high tree. He should tie a piece of cloth to the top. If there's any danger, pull the cloth down.'

'And you must put up a light in the ship,' said my wife. 'Then I'll know that you've got there safely.'

We reached the ship quite easily. The animals were in good

health and had enough food. I remembered my wife's words and put up a light. Then we had some food and went to sleep.

We woke up very early the next morning. We found useful things for our life on the island.

'We must have plenty of gunpowder,' said Fritz. 'Then we'll be safe if we meet wild animals or enemies. Later, we'll need . . .'

'We must think of the present,' I said. 'What do we need now, for these next few days or weeks? We must take more sailcloth because we need to make a home. And we must think of food. What food is there on the ship?'

'I've seen a barrel of butter,' said Fritz, 'and there's the ship's bread, and some meat in salt. But what will we do when the bread's finished? And the butter will soon go bad.'

'Let's think of the present,' I said. 'We have enough problems to worry about now. We can think about the future later. Perhaps a ship will come and take us away.'

But I was wrong. It's always a good idea to prepare for the future. We didn't know that at the time. So we made some silly mistakes. We didn't take back things that we needed later.

It was a slow job, getting all these things together. So we had to spend a second night on the ship.

◆

We woke up late the next morning.

'Now, Fritz,' I said, as we sat at breakfast, 'how can we take these animals to the land?'

'We can't put them in the boat,' he said. 'They're too heavy. Can we make another boat? No, the animals are too big. What can we do? The pig can swim, but the goats and the donkey can't swim so far.'

'No,' I said, 'we can't make a boat that's big enough. There are a lot of barrels on the ship – enough for a bigger boat. But we haven't got time to make one.'

'Barrels!' cried Fritz. 'Let's make a boat for each animal. Let's tie barrels to the animals. The barrels will hold them up above the water when we pull them behind the boat!'

'That's possible,' I said. 'Let's try first with one animal and see.'

We tied a barrel to each side of a sheep and put it into the sea. It went down and down...! Then finally I saw its head above the water, and it began to swim. When it was tired, it stopped swimming. It stayed there, held up by the barrels.

Fritz jumped into the sea and tied a rope to the sheep, and we pulled it back into the ship. We worked very hard and for a time the job seemed impossible. The pig and the donkey were the most difficult.

'Perhaps we should leave them,' said Fritz. 'We need the goats more than the other animals.'

We tied barrels to the goats, and then we tried again with the pig and the donkey. The donkey seemed to understand, but the pig gave us a lot of trouble.

'The pig's very fat,' said Fritz, 'and pigs are good swimmers. Perhaps its fat will keep it up in the water.' So we didn't tie barrels to the pig.

At last, we got all the animals into the water. Then we climbed into the boat and put up the sail.

◆

There was a strong wind, and we soon reached the land. I cut the barrels from the animals, and they came up on to the beach. They were glad to be on land again.

My wife and the boys came running. My wife was surprised to see all the animals, even the pig, safe on the land.

'How did you think of using the barrels?' she asked.

'I didn't think of it,' I answered. 'This was Fritz's plan, not mine.'

Chapter 5   A New Place

'What did you do, my dear, while Fritz and I were on the ship?' I asked.

'I found a place for our new home,' said my wife. 'It was impossible to stay in the tent because it was so hot. And there are no trees here that we can sit under. So Ernest and Jack took their guns, and we took enough food with us for the day. The dogs came too.

'We came to a river and crossed it on stones. Then we walked up to higher ground. From there, I could see a small group of ten or twelve trees. They were the biggest trees that I've ever seen. We stopped and ate our lunch there. It seemed to me to be the perfect place to live.

'There! Now you know my story! I went to look for a new place to live, and I found one. Promise me that we'll go there tomorrow. We'll make a home for ourselves in one of those big trees.'

'What!' I said, laughing. 'In a tree? A tree house! We can live *under* a tree, but how can we get up *into* the tree? Fly?'

'You can laugh if you want to. But I'm sure that we can build a small hut in the branches. We'll think of a way to get up there.'

'Right,' I said. 'We'll all go and see the place tomorrow. Then we'll think about what we can do.'

◆

During the night, I thought about our conversation. Then, as we sat at breakfast the next day, I said, 'Yes, we'll move to the place that you saw on the other side of the river.' I turned to the boys and said, 'Now, what's the first thing that we must do?'

'I know!' said Jack. 'We must move the tent there and then take all our things and the animals.'

'What do you think, Fritz?'

'The place is on the other side of the river. Mother, Ernest, Jack and Franz went across on stones. But the donkey and pig can't cross on those stones, and we can't carry our things across the water. We must build a bridge. That's the first thing, isn't it?'

'No,' said Ernest. 'First, we must go out to the ship and bring back wood for the bridge.'

'We don't have to do that,' said Jack. 'There was a lot of wood on the beach where that shellfish caught me. It's come from other ships, and there will be more there now.'

'Good boy!' I said. 'Let's see what we can find.'

Jack was right. We found plenty of wood. We tied together the big pieces which were useful to us. We pulled them to the mouth of the river. Then we got the donkey and, with its help, we pulled the pieces of wood up the river. Finally, they were at the place where we wanted to build our bridge.

It wasn't easy, but we put three long pieces across the river. Then we nailed more wood across them. It was very hard work, and we all slept well that night. The next morning, we got up early and began preparing for our journey.

We put our pots, food and smaller things into bags and hung them on each side of the donkey. We put little bags on the goats, but the pig refused to carry anything. Franz sat on the back of the donkey, so it could not run away. The boys and I carried the other things that we needed for the first few days in our new home.

When we were all ready, my wife said, 'We can't leave the chickens here. If we leave them, we'll lose them all.'

Fritz and Ernest tried to catch the chickens, but it was impossible. They ran away.

'I'll show you how to do it,' my wife said.

She threw a little corn on the ground, and all the chickens ran to it. When she threw some more inside the tent, they all went inside. Then, while they were eating, she closed the tent.

'Now, Jack, you go into the tent. Catch the birds and pass them out to us. We'll tie their legs and put them in two barrels on the donkey's back.'

◆

At last, we were ready to start. We put our other things inside the tent and closed it carefully.

Fritz and my wife went in front. Next came the donkey, with Franz on its back, then Jack with the goats. The monkey rode on the goat that gave him his milk. After him came Ernest and the sheep, and I came last. The dogs helped us to keep all the animals in line.

The pig did not want to come with us, so we left it behind. But when it saw us leaving, it came running after us. When we reached the bridge, it was there too!

We crossed the bridge very carefully. I was worried about the weight of the donkey, so I went first. The bridge was all right, so the donkey went next. Then the rest followed. But not the pig! Oh no! The pig refused to go on to the bridge.

We tried everything, but without success. Then, when we were all on the other side, the pig swam across. It followed us. So we reached the place where we wanted to make our new home.

'These are wonderful trees!' said Fritz. 'They're so tall!'

'Yes,' I said, 'I didn't think they were as big as this. This is an excellent place. If we can make a house in one of these trees, we'll be safe from wild animals.'

We tied up the animals so they couldn't escape – but not the pig. The pig lay down and slept. We freed the chickens, and my wife started a fire and cooked a meal for us.

Chapter 6   The Rope Ladder

After the meal, I said, 'We must sleep on the ground tonight. I can't see how we can get up into a tree this evening.'

Then I went to the beach with Fritz and Ernest. We looked for the things that we needed for a ladder. The beach was covered with pieces of wood of all sizes, carried there from ships by the sea.

'It'll be difficult to make a ladder out of these pieces of wood,' said Fritz. 'And it'll be very heavy.'

'Look at those tall thick plants there!' cried Ernest. 'They're what we need! Bamboo!'

I cut some bamboo into pieces about six feet long. Then I tied them together, so I could carry them. Then I cut some straight sticks.

'I can make a bow with this bamboo,' I said. 'And arrows from these sticks.'

We went back to the biggest tree, carrying the bamboo. We put it on the ground.

'That branch is about thirty feet high,' I said. 'We've got more than sixty feet of thick rope and a lot of thin rope. Now we'll put two long pieces of rope on the ground and we'll cut pieces of bamboo a foot and a half long. Fritz, you cut the pieces. Ernest will help me with the rope.'

So we began to work.

'Now,' I said, 'we must tie pieces of bamboo across the ropes to make steps. Then we'll have a rope ladder.'

We worked very hard, and after a few hours our ladder was ready. Then I made a bow from another piece of bamboo.

'Ernest,' I said, 'make arrows from these sticks. Put a big nail in one end.'

'Oh!' cried Jack. 'A bow and arrows! What are you going to do with them? I want to play with them!'

'I'm not making a toy, Jack. I'm going to shoot with this. But soon you'll all have bows and arrows, because we must be careful with our gunpowder. When we've used this gunpowder, we won't be able to get any more. And, if there are dangerous men on the island, we'll need our gunpowder.'

When the bow and arrows were ready, I tied a long piece of thin rope to an arrow and shot the arrow up over the branch. It came down on the other side, carrying the thin rope with it.

'Ah!' said Ernest — he always understood things quickly. 'You'll tie the rope ladder to this thin rope and pull it up on to the branch. Then you'll hold it there while someone ties it to the branch.'

'Yes,' I said. 'You climb up there. You're smaller than Fritz. And I don't think Jack can tie the ladder well enough.'

Soon the ladder was tied to the branch.

'That's a good day's work,' I said. 'Now we must tie up the animals, and we'll sleep at the foot of the tree. Tomorrow we'll begin to build our tree house.'

'Look!' said Jack. 'The chickens are on our rope ladder.'

I looked. Each chicken was sitting on a step. They were already very comfortable.

I lit a big fire to keep away dangerous animals. Then I decided to stay awake and watch.

Chapter 7   The Tree House

I was worried, at first. I didn't feel that we were in a very safe place. I heard a strange sound . . . No, it was only the movement of the trees. The fire was getting low . . . What were those shadows? Was that a wild animal moving nearer . . . nearer? I got up and put more wood on the fire. At last, I felt safer and went to sleep.

It was light when I woke up. All the others were already awake.

'Look!' said Jack. 'The chickens are on our rope ladder.'

We had breakfast, and then we started work again. My wife milked the goats. Then she went down to the beach with Ernest, Jack, Franz and the donkey to get wood for the tree house. Fritz and I climbed up the ladder into the tree, and planned our new home.

'These branches,' I said, 'are thick and close together, and they come straight out from the tree. The floor of the house can be here, and the tree will be one of the walls.'

Fritz looked up and said, 'Those higher branches will hold up the roof. But what sort of roof?'

'We'll put a sail over the branches and bring it down to the floor on two sides.'

That, as you will hear later, was a great mistake. I was very stupid! But at the time, Fritz and I were very pleased with our simple plans.

'This fourth side,' I said, 'will be open. We can look out from there. Perhaps we'll make a place where we can sit outside in the daytime.'

'It'll be a beautiful house!' said Fritz.

Then my wife and Ernest arrived. The donkey was pulling a lot of wood behind it. More wood was tied on its back, and Franz was sitting on top of that. They left the wood and went back for more.

'How shall we get it up here?' said Fritz. 'Shall I carry it up the ladder?'

'No, we must pull it up. Now where did I see . . .? Yes, I remember. It was in Ernest's box of tools.'

Fritz found the little wheel. We tied it to a branch and pulled up the pieces of wood. Then I started to make the floor.

◆

When evening came, the floor was finished. We hung our sailcloth over the higher branches and nailed it down to the floor on two sides. On the fourth side, we could see across the country round us, and plenty of air could come into the house.

'There!' I said. 'Our house is finished.' Then I saw that there were more pieces of wood. 'We'll make a table and some chairs from these tomorrow. Tonight we'll sleep in our new house.'

The three older boys quickly went up the ladder, carrying everything for their beds. My wife was afraid of the ladder, but she reached the top safely. Then I took Franz on my back. I untied the ladder from the posts in the ground, climbed up and pulled the ladder up after me.

'Now we're safe in our Tree House,' said Jack. 'Nothing can climb up here!'

'Oh!' cried Fritz. 'Where's the monkey?'

'There!' said Ernest, pointing to Fritz's bed. 'A monkey can climb up anywhere!'

I kept my gun by my side. I was still not sure that the animals below were safe. But the night passed quietly.

Chapter 8   Back to the Tent

After breakfast, Fritz and I started to make a table. Suddenly, we heard a loud BANG, and a small bird fell almost at our feet.

'That was a good shot!' said Ernest, picking it up. He was very proud.

'It wasn't good,' I said. 'We can't use our gunpowder like that. We can use the guns to shoot large animals for food. But for birds and small animals, we must use bows and arrows. Look at the bow and arrow that I've made, Ernest. Try to make better ones – and learn to use them.'

◆

When midday came, we put some barrels round the new table. We were ready to eat our first meal at it.

'Where are Ernest and Jack?' asked my wife.

'Let's start. If they come late, they won't have any lunch.'

'Maybe something has happened to them,' said my wife. 'I can't eat if they're not here.'

We waited.

'I'm sure nothing has happened to them,' I said at last. 'They're young and silly and don't notice the time. Put the food on the table.'

Then Ernest and Jack arrived, carrying bows and arrows.

'Look!' said Jack, before I could speak. He held out two very small birds. 'We shot them with our bows and arrows!'

'I'm very pleased about that. But I'm angry because you're late. Your mother's been worried about you. Sit down and eat your lunch.'

We only had meat and a little bread for lunch. The bread was very hard. The meat was an animal that I shot the day before.

'I left some things at the tent,' said my wife. 'If we get them, I can give you better meals.'

◆

We left and walked towards the beach. The dogs went in front; this time, the little monkey was riding on Turk's back. Then came Fritz, Ernest and Jack with their bows and arrows. My wife and Franz and I came last. There was still a lot of wood on the beach, and I noticed two long pieces, just the same shape. Their ends were turned up.

'Now where,' I thought, 'have I seen pieces of wood shaped like that? Ah! I remember! In Switzerland, of course!'

We reached the tent and found everything in the same place as before. Everyone looked for the things that they wanted. Fritz got some gunpowder, while I found the butter. My wife pointed to a bag that I remembered putting into our boat.

'What is it?' I asked.

'Ah!' she said. 'That's what I wanted for our lunch. Potatoes!'

'There are only enough for one meal,' I said. 'But if we plant them, we'll have plenty next year – enough for all our meals.'

Jack was listening to this. 'We can eat these potatoes and then we can find wild potatoes,' he said. 'You found sugar and coconuts.'

'No, Jack. Wild potatoes grow on the top of high mountains. And they're very small and not very good to eat. These potatoes are different from wild ones. We must make a garden and grow potatoes in it.'

'But what can we eat now?' asked Jack.

'I'll see what I can find,' I answered, 'until our garden's ready. There are some wild plants that we can use.'

Next, Fritz and I went to get salt. The sea water dried on the rocks and left salt behind. We were able to get enough to give our food some taste. But we were stupid not to take more than that!

Chapter 9   The Sledge

Later in bed, I thought, 'That barrel of butter was very heavy. We must find a way to carry heavy things.' I thought about our animals, tied up at the foot of the tree at night. They weren't safe. We must make huts for them. We needed wood for this, but more than we used for the floor of our house. We also needed bamboo.

The donkey couldn't carry so much, so we must make a sledge. Those two pieces of wood on the beach were just the right shape for the bottom of a sledge.

So early in the morning, Ernest and I climbed quietly down the ladder. I took some tools, nails and a piece of light rope. We found the two pieces of wood, and nailed them together with smaller pieces. Then we put a lot of bamboo and wood across the

20

top. I tied a rope on the front, and we pulled the sledge back along the beach. It moved very easily across the sand.

◆

When we were finishing our breakfast, we heard a loud noise from the chickens. We all ran to them.

'It's the monkey!' cried Ernest, 'He's running after them.'

Then we saw the monkey hiding behind a tree. He was eating an egg. The monkey ran away to another tree, and Ernest ran after him. Soon Ernest came back with four more eggs. My wife went and looked in the grass.

'One of the chickens is sitting on her eggs,' she said. 'Soon we'll have some little ones. We must make a safe place for the chickens. Then we can keep the monkey away from them.'

◆

After lunch, Ernest and I went out again with the donkey. The donkey pulled the sledge to the beach. We put more wood and bamboo on the sledge, and then I looked at the sky.

'We must go home,' I said. 'There are clouds in the sky, and the wind is getting stronger.'

Then I looked at the place where the ship was still on the rocks. Another storm could carry the rest of it away. We must make one more journey to the ship before it broke into pieces. Why was I so stupid on our last journey? We brought back the animals, butter, salt meat, bedclothes, gunpowder, some books. But we knew then that we were on the island for a long time – a year, two years . . . perhaps for the rest of our lives. Why didn't I think of other, more important things?

The donkey pulled the sledge to the beach.

Chapter 10   A Second Journey to the Ship

The next morning, Fritz and I got up very early. We went to look at our boat. It was in a good state, but it didn't have a sail. That was now the Tree House roof.

'I think,' said Fritz, 'that we can use long flat pieces of wood as paddles.'

'Yes,' I said, 'but we must get another sail from the ship. The boat will be very heavy with everything in it. There's still a strong wind. We'll run back home and tell the others. We'll go now, and then we'll spend the night on the ship.'

We went quickly and told them our plans. My wife said, 'We'll meet you with the sledge when you come back. Be careful!'

◆

We reached the ship without great problems.

'Now, Fritz, what do we really need?'

'I can only think of one very small thing,' he answered.

'What's that?'

'I want something to catch big fish.'

'Yes,' I said, 'but we can't eat fish and meat every day.'

'No,' he answered. 'We must have bread, and fruit, and green vegetables.'

'Do you remember Mr Wilkins, on the ship? He was moving to a new home. I'll see if I can find his tools. You find a fishing line.'

'Yes,' said Fritz. 'I remember watching one of the officers when he was fishing over the side of the boat. I know which room was his. I'll look there.'

I went below and found some gardening tools. I also found some seeds. 'That's lucky!' I thought. 'Now we'll have lots of different vegetables to eat.'

Fritz came back with his arms full.

'I remember,' I said to Fritz, 'that Mr Wilkins was bringing a light plough with him. Shall I take the plough to the island?'

'What will pull it?' asked Fritz. 'I don't think the donkey can pull a plough.'

'No,' I answered, 'no, you're right. But it isn't very big. We'll take it. Perhaps we can use it.'

◆

We slept on the ship that night. The next day was windier, and the sky looked stormy. We put a good sail on our boat and started back towards the land.

'Perhaps,' said Fritz, 'we can catch a fish on the way back to the land.'

He put a fishing line over the side and pulled it through the water. Suddenly, we felt something on the line. It was very strong – it pulled the boat back towards the open sea.

'The fish will carry us away!' cried Fritz.

'We must cut the line,' I said.

'No, no!' cried Fritz. 'Let's wait.'

Just then, the wind began, and it pushed the boat towards the land. It became stronger and stronger, and we moved faster and faster through the water. The boat was thrown up on to the beach and it broke into pieces.

◆

My wife and the boys were waiting for us. We quickly took our things off the boat and put them on the sledge.

'There! That's all,' I said.

'No,' answered Fritz. 'No! Let's see if the fish is still with us.' He went into the water. 'Yes, it's still here. It's dead.' So we carried the big fish on to the beach and put it on the sledge.

'This will give us food for days,' I said, 'if it doesn't go bad. We must put it in salt.'

'But now,' said Ernest, 'we haven't got a boat. What shall we do?'

'We'll take the barrels that we used for the boat,' I said. 'They'll be very useful for food and other things. Ernest, you walk along the beach. I think the sea threw one of the ship's boats out of the water there.'

I was right. There was a boat there. It was badly broken, but we were able to mend it.

We had some of the fish for supper, and it tasted very nice. Then my wife kept some for our meals the next day, and put the rest into a barrel with salt.

◆

After our meal, we sat round the fire. We talked about the things that we had to do in the next few days.

'You must make a hut for the tools and other large things,' said my wife. 'You can't carry those tools up and down into our house.'

'Yes,' I said, 'and we must also make some huts for the animals.'

'We won't need many huts,' said Ernest.

'Oh?' I said. 'Let's see. I think we'll have more animals soon.' And I was right!

'We must make a garden too,' I said.

'A big garden!' said Fritz. 'What have we got? Plants and seeds from the ship – and potatoes. And perhaps we can find other plants on the island that we can grow in our garden.'

'Yes,' I said, 'but we must build a wall round the garden. We don't want the animals to eat the plants. We'll use bamboo.'

'Oh, that's a lot of work!' said Ernest. Ernest was lazy and didn't like work.

'There's one thing that you haven't told me,' said my wife. 'You've told me what we'll be able to eat next year. But what are we going to eat now?'

'Ah,' I said. 'We haven't got any potatoes, but there are wild plants. I'm sure that there are sweet potatoes on this island.'

◆

Next morning, we all went out and looked for sweet potatoes. For some time, we didn't find anything. Then Fritz found a plant and called me.

'Is this a sweet potato?' he asked.

'Yes,' I said. 'It is.'

We looked around and found more.

Back at the Tree House, my wife cooked the sweet potatoes. They tasted like potatoes, but not as nice. Then she made some of the potatoes into a sort of bread. It was quite hard, but good.

Chapter 11   The Garden

We got up very early in the morning. We wanted to start work on our garden before the weather got hot. Fritz, Ernest and I took our tools. Jack had a fork, but he wasn't really old enough.

We all started to work. After a time, when we were quite tired, I said, 'Let's see what the animals left on the ground last night. That'll be very good for the earth in the garden.'

We went to look.

'The pig! The pig's gone!' Jack cried.

It was true – the pig was nowhere near the Tree House.

'We can't do anything about that,' I said. 'Perhaps she'll come back again.'

'You said "she"?' said Jack.

'Yes, of course. I think she's going to be a mother. Perhaps she's gone away to the forest to have her babies there. Then she'll come back, I hope.'

We went back and worked again in the garden. We were all

very tired when it was time for the evening meal. We had fish and sweet potatoes.

'Now,' I said, 'we must work in the garden again tomorrow, and plant all the seeds from the ship. Then we'll put bamboo around our garden and make huts for the animals.'

'We must make a big hut for the pig,' said Jack, 'if she has a lot of little pigs.'

'Now, go to bed,' I said to the boys. 'Be ready to work hard tomorrow. First, we'll get the bamboo.'

'How will we carry a lot of bamboo across the ground?' asked Jack. 'We can't use the sledge. Can the donkey pull it?'

'No,' I said. 'We won't go to the place where we found bamboo before. We'll go to a different place. Then we'll be able to bring it here more easily.'

'Oh,' said Jack, 'is there an easier way?'

'Yes,' I said, 'we'll go up the river. We'll cut the pieces of bamboo and pull them to the river. Then the river can carry them down to our Tree House.'

'Ah!' said Jack. 'Yes, that'll be the best way.'

Chapter 12   Buffaloes and Other Animals

We left the next morning to get bamboo for our garden and for animal huts. My wife and the four boys came with me and the two dogs, Turk and Flora. We also took the donkey. We needed it to pull the bamboo to the side of the river. It was our first visit to this part of the island, so we took our guns with us. The dogs were a mistake – but the guns weren't.

We went up the river and found a lot of bamboo. We cut it and tied it together, and the donkey pulled it to the river. Then we had a meal and rested.

Jack went for a walk. After a time, he came back and said,

'Father, there's a big field over there, and there are ten or fifteen large horses in it.'

I said, 'Jack, there aren't any horses in this place.'

'There are!' he said. 'Come and see.'

When we came out of the trees, we saw a lot of buffaloes. We went nearer and nearer until we were about 130 feet away. The buffaloes stood and looked at us with their big round eyes. They didn't seem to be angry or afraid. I could see two young buffaloes.

Then Turk and Flora began to jump up and down, making a lot of noise. The buffaloes became angry, and they came towards us. We were in great danger, but Fritz and I both used our guns. One of the buffaloes fell dead, and the others turned and ran away. We were lucky to escape so easily.

I said to Fritz and Ernest, 'Come and catch those two young buffaloes. The dogs have pushed them into the trees. We must take them with us.'

We put ropes round their necks, and they came with us without any trouble. We hurried away as fast as we could.

'Now,' I said, 'we'll leave the bamboo until tomorrow. But the young buffaloes will be very useful! We'll give them milk from the goat.'

◆

The goat gave the young buffaloes her milk.

'But,' said Jack, 'there won't be much milk for us.'

'No,' I said, 'but soon we'll have as much milk as we need.'

'You seem very pleased about the young buffaloes,' said Ernest.

'Yes, I am,' I answered, 'because now I can see an answer to two big problems.'

'Oh,' said Ernest, 'what problems?'

'These,' I answered. 'When the goat doesn't give us any more milk, we won't have any. But these two young buffaloes will

When we came out of the trees, we saw a lot of buffaloes.

grow up, and they'll have babies. So we'll have more and more buffaloes and plenty of milk. Buffalo milk is very good. We can make butter from it, and perhaps cheese too.'

'And what was the other problem?' asked Fritz.

'The other problem?' I answered. 'You remember the plough that we brought from the ship? I didn't know how we could pull it. A buffalo is very strong and the buffaloes can pull the plough for us. So now we have a plough and we have milk.'

'Not yet,' said Ernest.

'No, not yet,' I answered, 'but next year. We mustn't think only of today. We must think of future years.'

◆

The next day, we went back and cut up the dead buffalo. We brought a lot of the meat back and put it into barrels with salt. 'Now,' I thought, 'we'll have food in the winter.' We also put the bamboo in the river, and the river carried it down to a place near the Tree House. We pulled it to the Tree House and started to put it around our garden.

◆

Some days later, when the garden was finished, I said, 'Now we must begin to make huts for the animals.'

'We'll only need three huts,' said Ernest.

'Why only three huts?' I asked.

'We need one for the buffaloes, one for the goats and another for the sheep,' said Ernest. 'And perhaps we should make a house for the chickens.'

'But,' I said, 'the donkey and the pig need huts too.'

'Oh,' said Ernest, 'the pig's gone. And today the donkey's gone too.'

'Gone?' I said.

'Yes. I can't see it anywhere. And the pig went days ago.'

'Yes,' I said, 'but I hope they'll come back. We'll make huts for all of them, and hope.'

◆

We were sitting at breakfast, a few days later, when Fritz said, 'Something's moving in those tall grasses. I'll get my gun.'

He ran and got his gun.

'Wait!' I said. 'Don't shoot. Let's see what it is.'

Jack said, 'I'll go round behind it and look. If it's dangerous, I'll run away.'

So Jack moved very quietly. He was very good at that because he often followed birds with his bow and arrow. The thing came nearer – and then out came our pig with six little ones!

'At last!' I said. 'We're all very glad to see you, Mrs Pig. And your house is ready for you!'

So we pushed the pig and her six babies into their hut.

Then Franz called to me. 'Look!' he cried. 'Flora's had six babies too!'

So now we had eight dogs and seven pigs.

'Now where's our donkey?' I said.

◆

One morning, we were planting potatoes in the garden, when we heard a strange noise.

'What's that?' I said. 'What sort of animal is making that noise?'

The dogs heard it too. They looked ready for a fight. We all looked round. We couldn't see anything, but the noise continued. It came nearer and nearer, and our dogs became angrier and angrier. I tied them to a tree.

Then Fritz put down his gun and started to laugh. 'I can see it,' he said. 'It's our donkey. He's come back!'

There he was. And then we saw that he wasn't alone. Our

31

donkey was bringing another animal with him, very similar to a donkey but smaller.

'That,' I said to Jack and Ernest, 'is probably a kind of wild donkey. Now don't make a sound. Fritz and I will try to catch her.'

Fritz moved towards our donkey, holding some salt in his hand. Our donkey loved salt. He came to Fritz, and the wild donkey came a little closer too. Then, when she was near enough, I put a rope over her head from behind her. She fought against us, but at last we were able to tie her up.

I said, 'Perhaps the wild donkey will have babies. It will be easier to teach her if she does. And she'll be useful to us.' And that is what happened, in the end.

The chickens were sitting on eggs, and soon we had forty little ones. So now we had a lot of animals to feed. We had the donkey and the wild donkey, two buffaloes, the goats, the pigs and the dogs, the sheep and the monkey.

I said, 'We must work very hard and get food for all these animals. The rainy season is coming.'

So we brought the tent from the beach and filled it with dry grass. We got sweet potatoes and coconuts and put them in a dry place at the foot of the tree.

Chapter 13   Winter

There were dark clouds in the sky, and the sea was stormy. I looked out to sea and thought, 'The sea has finally broken up our ship. There will be more wood on the beach. And this rough sea will come up to our boat on the beach.'

'Boys,' I said, 'we must pull our boat high up on the beach. We don't want the sea to carry it away. And we must turn it over, so it doesn't fill with water.'

We went down to the beach and pulled the boat up high on

the sand and turned it over.

Then Ernest pointed and said, 'What's that thing there? That square thing?'

I looked and saw a big box. It was nearly covered with sand. We uncovered it and opened it, and it was full of a sailor's clothes. The clothes were very wet and salty from the sea water.

'We can wash them in the river and dry them,' I said.

'They'll be too big for us,' said Jack. 'They're too big for Fritz, or Ernest.'

'Yes,' I said, 'they'll be too big for you. But you'll be glad when your other clothes have got wet in the rain.'

Then I thought, 'Now winter's coming, what do we need? Dry firewood for my wife to cook with under the Tree House.'

We didn't, of course, cook *in* the Tree House, because of the wooden floor. So we found a lot of firewood and put it at the foot of the tree, under the Tree House.

Then I thought, 'In the stormy weather we won't be able to go far from our house to get food. We must be sure that we have a lot of food in or near the house. Then we can use that when the weather's very bad. We've got barrels of salt meat and buffalo meat. I hope it will keep well. We can't get any more salt.'

The sea was now coming up over the rocks. And there was no sunshine to dry the salt.

My thoughts continued, 'We've got eggs, of course, from our chickens. Perhaps we can catch fish with the fishing line from the ship. But that's not easy when the sea is very stormy. We've got sweet potatoes and a lot of coconuts. The goats will give us a little milk, and there's plenty of dry grass for our animals.'

'Now,' I said to my family, 'we've got a good house and plenty of food, so we're ready for the winter.'

That's what I thought. But I was very wrong!

◆

The next few months were probably the unhappiest months that I have ever known in all my life. We had four enemies – the rain, the wind, the cold and the shorter days. The days were not much shorter, but we had to spend a lot of time inside the house because of the bad weather.

The rain came down like a river from the sky. It rained nearly all day and all night. There were only a few days when it stopped. Most of the land was under water. The river was too big to cross, and our bridge was broken. Luckily our garden was on higher ground, and our plants were beginning to come through.

The wind was very strong. When we made our Tree House, I didn't think about the wind. If a house is built on the ground, with good walls and a low roof, the wind will pass over it. The house is safe. But when a house is built up in a tree, the wind goes up into it.

The roof of our house was made of sailcloth. When it rained, there were deep pools of water on the roof. The water ran over the sides, on to the floor. Then the strong wind pushed the sailcloth up, and a river of rain came down into the room!

The days were not as hot as before, and the nights were the same – sometimes even cold. We sat all day in wet clothes and we couldn't dry them. In the evenings, we didn't know how to keep warm. We put stones on the floor of our tree room and lit a fire on them, but soon the room was full of smoke and we were afraid of a fire. We couldn't get the smoke out of the room. We couldn't make a hole in the roof because of the rain.

When the sun went down, darkness came suddenly. But even in the daytime, the room was quite dark. We had no light. We burned small pieces of wood, giving a little light. But that wasn't enough. So at night we sat round in our wet clothes, very cold, in the darkness. There was nothing to do except sleep.

◆

When it rained, there were deep pools of water on the roof.

We couldn't continue like this.

I said, 'We must go down and live at the foot of the tree. We'll put a sailcloth over this floor. Then there will be two roofs – the roof in the tree and the roof on this floor. Then we'll be dry down there.'

We built two walls at the foot of the tree. The animals' huts made the third wall, and the tree was the fourth wall. We made a hole in the floor of the upstairs room for the smoke from our fire. Now the rain couldn't come straight down on to the fire.

We were more comfortable in this lower room, but the smell of the animals came in from the huts, and that was terrible.

◆

After a time, we began to have problems with our food. The buffalo meat went bad because there wasn't enough salt in the barrels. Oh, why didn't I think about that before? We needed a lot of salt to keep our food fresh through the bad months of the year.

We killed some of the older chickens and ate them. Then, when the weather was better, the boys were able to go out fishing or shooting with their bows and arrows. They brought in a little fish and meat. We had sweet potatoes, but cooking was very difficult. When the weather was good, my wife made enough sweet-potato bread for a few days. But it wasn't very good.

We didn't have enough food for the animals. We killed four of the young dogs, leaving only Turk and Flora and two of their babies. We had to find food for the goats, the sheep and the buffaloes. We couldn't give them enough food in their huts, so we moved them out into the forest. We put coconut shells around their necks, so we could hear them. Then we put a little food in their huts each night, so they wanted to come back home.

Chapter 14   The Cave House

We were very pleased when the storms ended. After those long weeks of rain, the sun shone again. We came out from our dark, smelly room and looked up at the bright sun. Around us the grass was green, and flowers were coming through. In our garden, the plants were coming up very well – but the birds saw them too! So Jack guarded them, with Flora's help, and kept the birds away. We also put fishing lines across the plants to protect them from those little thieves.

We hung up our clothes in the sunlight to dry them. Then we started work on the Tree House. In a few days, we were able to leave our room at the foot of the tree and go back to our bright and happy home.

'I can't live through another winter like that,' said my wife. 'It will kill me. I'm sure that the first men, thousands of years ago, didn't live in trees like monkeys. They lived in caves, and we must find one too.'

I knew that she was right. I went out and walked along the coast and looked at the hills near the sea. Some came straight down to the beach. Those were possible places for caves. I walked a long way, but I couldn't see any big ones. I needed a large cave for my family.

I went back and told my wife and the boys. The caves weren't large enough for us.

'So,' said Fritz, 'if the caves aren't big enough, we must make one bigger.'

'You can try,' I said, 'but the rock's very hard. I don't know if it's possible. I'll take you to the best cave that I've found, above the beach. It was probably made by the sea, but the sea's gone down and left it in the side of the hill. Bring the tools and we'll try.'

◆

So we went to the cave. We worked for a week, but we only made the cave six feet deeper. The rock was very hard. I thought about using gunpowder, but gunpowder was too important for us. I didn't know what to do.

'Shall we stop?' I asked Fritz. 'Shall we think of another idea?'

'I think,' said Fritz, 'that the rock is getting softer. This piece here seems softer.'

Jack was the smallest, so he was working at the lowest part of the rock. One morning, he cried out, 'I've done it! I've done it! I've made a hole right through the rock!'

'Don't be so silly,' said Fritz. 'I don't believe you.'

'But I have!' said Jack, 'I have!'

Fritz went to look. He soon came back, saying, 'It's true, Father. Jack's right. I can't understand it. Jack has made a hole in the rock and there's nothing behind it.'

I was very surprised. I took a long piece of bamboo and put it through the hole.

'Yes,' I said, 'there's nothing behind there.'

'Let's make the hole bigger,' said Fritz. 'Then one of us can go through.'

I said, 'That's dangerous. If the hole's very deep, you'll fall. We must be very careful. Let's make the hole a little bigger. Then I can put my head in and look.'

So we made the hole bigger and I put my head in. Suddenly, I felt very ill. I moved away.

'You mustn't go into the cave, boys – if it's a cave,' I said. 'The air's really bad and dangerous. I'm sure you can die in there. First, we must drive out the bad air.'

'How can we do that?' asked Fritz.

'We must light a fire,' I replied.

So we put burning grass and sticks into the hole, but the fire went out immediately.

'Perhaps,' said Ernest, 'if we light a fire just in front of the hole, the hot air will pull the cold air out of the cave.'

'Yes, that's possible,' I said. 'But I think that will be slow – and, perhaps, dangerous. I think this time we should use some of our gunpowder.'

So I took some coconut shells, tied some rope round them and filled them with gunpowder. Then I lit one and threw it quickly into the cave. There was a very loud noise, and the bad air came out with the smoke. I did the same with two more coconut shells and then we tried to light a fire again.

This time the fire burned. It didn't burn very well, but the smoke and hot air came out through the hole and soon the fire was burning better. At last, it began to burn brightly – as brightly inside the cave as in the open air.

'Run to the Tree House,' I said to Ernest. 'Bring all the small pieces of wood that we've got. We can use them as lights when we go into the cave.'

While he was gone, we made the mouth of the cave bigger. Then we could see the walls that were nearest the doorway. Jack looked in and said, 'The walls are covered with beautiful stones in lots of different colours. It's wonderful!'

I looked into the cave. Jack was right. The walls were covered with things that looked like stones.

'That's very strange,' I said. 'What are they?'

Then Ernest came back from the Tree House, bringing the wood. I went into the cave first. I wanted to be sure that the air was good. I looked at the stones. Some were lying on the floor because of the gunpowder. I took one and tasted it. It was salt. Salt!

'Look, boys,' I cried. 'We'll never have to look for salt again! Next winter we'll have plenty of salt, and we'll have meat through all the bad months.'

We looked round the cave. It was very big. I saw that we could make a room at one end for all our things, with a bedroom next to it. We could have another big room as a kitchen and sitting room.

'But,' I said, 'there's one thing that we must make now. I don't think this end of the cave is very far from the outside air. I'll hit the rock inside the cave. I want you, Fritz, to go outside and listen. Tell me where you hear me most clearly. Put a stick there to show the place.'

So Fritz went out and I started to knock on the inside of the cave wall in different places. After a time, he came back and said, 'I've found the best place. I can hear you quite well.'

'Ah!' I said. 'Then we'll make a hole through there from the outside. We need fresh air in the cave. It'll be hard work, but we must do it.'

◆

It *was* hard work, but after two days Fritz was able to put bamboo through the hole. The other end of it came into the cave. Then we made the hole bigger from inside the cave.

'Now,' I said, 'we can make a fireplace, with a hole for the smoke.'

So we started work, using stones and earth. We made a good fireplace, with a hole for the smoke.

'Now,' I said, 'we'll see if this idea really works.'

So we lit a fire, but the smoke came out into the cave. I saw that the boys were very sad. They thought that all their work was for nothing.

'No,' I said, 'don't worry. When the hole gets warm, the air will go up it. It'll be all right. Keep the fire going for two days, and it'll work very well.'

And that was what happened. On the second evening, the air began to go up the hole and it took all the smoke out of the cave.

'Now,' I said, 'we don't have to fear the next winter.'

My wife was very pleased. She said, 'Now I can cook and dry

your clothes, and we can sit round a nice bright fire on winter evenings. We'll be very happy.'

'Yes,' I said, 'but we'll have to do a lot more work. Next winter we'll have more animals. We must build a farm between the Tree House and the cave. Then the animals can live there in the summer *and* winter.'

'And we'll need a lot more food,' said Fritz.

'Yes,' I said. 'We can use the plough to make fields, and we must grow lots of vegetables. To work! To work!'

◆

So we all had a very busy summer. We put lots of salt meat, dried fish and coconuts in the cave. When the end of the year came, we added potatoes and sweet potatoes. Then we made a hut at the farm, and put dried grass and other food in it for the animals. We built a small hut there for someone to live in. They could look after the farm at night and drive away wild animals.

'What are we going to do about clothes?' asked my wife. 'The boys' clothes are in a terrible state, and the clothes from the sailor's box aren't very useful. When we found them, they were full of sea water. Now they're falling to pieces. They'll be all right for another year, but not longer. I must make cloth.'

'How can you make cloth?' said Fritz. 'From what? We've only got two sheep.'

'There are plants,' I said, 'that we can use for cloth.'

I won't tell you about all our problems with those plants. But in the end, my wife was able to make cloth. It wasn't very good and it wasn't very white, but she was happy. But until then the boys wore animal skins. They caught the animals, and we now had plenty of salt. So we prepared the skins, and my wife was able to make clothes out of them.

◆

So the year passed – our second year on the island. The boys were getting big and strong. Fritz was now nearly sixteen, and Ernest was fourteen. I thought about the future.

One evening, I said to them, 'You two are the oldest. Soon I'll have two fine, strong men to help me in our work on the island. As I become older, you'll be able to do the harder work. Jack is a quick learner and he can help your mother. Little Franz isn't very helpful yet, but he's a good little boy and doesn't give us much trouble. Yes, we're very lucky.'

Chapter 15   The Canoe

As the years passed, we made our houses better. We put a wooden roof on the Tree House. The rain didn't come through in winter after that, but it still wasn't a good home for the rainy season. We also built a place in front of the cave. We could sit out there and enjoy the sea air and the sunlight.

The farm became bigger and bigger. The buffaloes pulled the plough and they gave us all our milk. We were able to make butter from it too.

We got more eggs from our chickens than we could eat in the spring and the summer. In the winter, we had just enough eggs for our needs. The wild donkey had a baby. It was very pretty and it was easier to teach than its mother.

◆

Of course we had problems. One morning, Jack came running back from the farm. 'Oh Father, Father, come and see!' he cried.

I went down there. Everything in the farm buildings was broken, and the plants from the fields were everywhere. Monkeys laughed at us from the trees.

'Oh no!' I said. 'They've destroyed everything. We must be sure that this never happens again.'

Turk and Flora's babies were now old enough for us to teach them. We made a rule that one of us – Fritz, Ernest or I – always slept down at the farm with the dogs. They were quick to learn about the monkeys. We showed them that they must always run after a monkey. When they did, the monkeys ran away. Soon the monkeys stopped coming to the farm.

◆

As I watched my boys grow up, I was very pleased with them. Fritz was very strong and tall. Ernest wasn't as big, and he was quieter. But he wasn't as lazy as before. He wrote down the names of all the plants on the island and drew pictures of them. He made some paper out of plants, like the Egyptians many thousands of years ago. Franz was more sensible than Jack. He always did what he promised to do. But Jack was a good son too, and he did a lot of work on the farm. Franz liked helping his mother, while Jack spent more time with me.

◆

One day, Fritz said to me, 'I'd like to go away alone. I want to visit the parts of the island that we haven't seen. The ship's boat is too heavy for one person. I want to make a canoe.'

'I think we can make a canoe,' I said. 'I've seen canoes made from the bark of tall trees. I'll try to help you.'

We found a big tree and I cut a ring round the bark, at the bottom. Then I tied a rope ladder to one of the branches. I told Fritz to cut round the tree about twenty feet up from the ring. Then I made a cut from top to bottom between the two circles. We took the bark off very carefully, and it fell away in one piece.

We tied pieces of bamboo to our canoe to hold it in the right shape. Then we nailed together the sides at each end of the boat. A sweet juice from one of the trees dried quickly and went hard. We used this to fill the holes.

'I think,' said Fritz, 'that the water will come in over the front of the canoe, and perhaps over the back. Perhaps we should cover those places. We can leave a place in the middle where I can sit.'

'Yes,' I said, 'you're right. We must put a light cover over it.'

We also found a long flat piece of wood. Fritz could use that as a paddle, to move the boat along.

When the canoe was ready, we waited for a few days. Then it was dry, and we tried it in the water. At first, Fritz had problems in the canoe. It turned over and he often fell out. But he practised, and after a few days he was able to travel safely, even in rough sea.

Chapter 16   Jenny

One day, Fritz went away in his little canoe. He stayed away all day. In the evening, my wife became very worried.

'I'm afraid that something has happened to him,' she said.

We couldn't do anything, so we went to bed. But we didn't sleep very much. The next day, we went up to the top of a hill, but we couldn't see him. Then Ernest pointed.

'Look!' he said. 'Is that him?'

We looked. It was Fritz in his canoe. We all ran down to the water to meet him.

'Oh, Fritz,' cried his mother, 'I thought you were dead.'

While he was having breakfast, Fritz told us his story.

'I've always wanted to know more about the west of the island, so I decided to look there. I took my gun and some gunpowder, a fishing line and my knife. I came to the place where we found shellfish for the first time. I went for a swim

At first, Fritz had problems in the canoe.

there, and I found a lot more. I brought some up on to the beach and opened them. Inside one of them I found this.' He held out his hand. In it there was a large pearl. 'I opened some more and I found a lot of pearls. Look!'

'If you make holes through them, Mother can wear them around her neck,' said Jack.

'No, no,' said my wife, 'I don't want them. Who wants to wear pearls on this island?'

'Perhaps one day,' I said, 'a ship will come and take you home. You can sell these for a lot of money. We'll put them in a safe place.'

'I haven't told you the most important thing,' said Fritz. 'I went on farther to the west. In the evening, I sat on the beach and had a meal. As I was sitting there, a big bird flew over me. It was flying very slowly, so I shot it. Then I saw why it was flying so slowly. It was hurt. And this was tied around its leg.'

He showed us a little piece of cloth with writing on it.

I looked at the writing: 'Help! Sailor on smoking island.'

'The person wrote the message in blood!' I said.

'Yes,' said Fritz, 'but where is the smoking island? I went up the hill behind me and I looked out to sea. There, far out at sea, there was a little smoke going into the sky. It came from a small island.

'I went out to the island and climbed up to the top. In a little wood, I saw a small hut made of branches. In front of the hut there was a fire, and fish was cooking in a big shell. I hid behind a tree and waited. Then someone came out of the hut. She was wearing the coat of a ship's officer. She went to the fire. I came out of the trees and she turned round.'

'She!' I said. 'Did you say "she"?'

'Yes. It was a young woman! I told her not to be afraid. I told her about us. She can live with us, can't she? We will bring her here, won't we?'

'Yes, of course we will. But tell us about her.'

'Her father's William Montrose, an officer who lives in India. Her mother died when she was born. Her father was going back to England in a ship with his men, so Jenny had to travel in another ship. Her ship was lost in a storm a year ago.

'She got away in a boat with a ship's officer and some sailors. The officer gave her his coat. He told her to watch for another ship or for land. Then another storm came. A big wave covered the boat . . . She doesn't know what happened after that. When she opened her eyes, she was on that little island.'

'How has she lived there for more than a year?'

'I asked her that. She's got shellfish, and there are coconuts on the trees. She made a fishing line from her hair and she catches small fish. She uses stones to make a fire. She's made a little hut for birds from bamboo, but she can only catch small ones. When the big bird came down on the island, it hurt its leg. So she was able to tie that piece of cloth round it, with her call for help.'

'And the bird came to you.'

'Yes,' said Fritz. 'I sat with her and listened to her story. Then I told her to stay on the island. I promised to return as quickly as possible. I couldn't come all the way home that day. I slept on the beach and started again this morning. Can we go to Jenny today?'

'Yes,' I said, 'yes, if we start immediately.'

◆

I asked my wife to make preparations for Jenny. Then, taking a day's food with us, Fritz and I left in the ship's boat.

Jenny was waving from the beach as we came near. We stepped out of the boat onto the beach, and she threw her arms round my neck and cried.

We sailed back home along the coast. Mother and the three

47

Jenny was waving from the beach as we came near.

boys were waiting on the beach to meet Jenny.

My wife said, 'I'll have to dress you like one of my sons, because these are our only clothes.'

Jenny had a bath and dressed in sailors' clothes. Then she joined us for a large lunch, and Jack put flowers in her hair.

◆

Perhaps my boys thought that they could teach Jenny a lot of things. But she could shoot better than they could.

'My father taught me in India,' she said.

She was very good at catching fish. She was able to tell Ernest the real names of many of his plants.

'I learned all that at school,' she told him.

Very soon she and the boys were close friends.

Jenny thought about her father all the time. 'I'm sure that ships are looking for me,' she said.

Fritz said, 'If a ship comes, we'll hear a gun. We'll answer with our guns. Then they'll know that we're here.'

'A ship *will* come one day and take me back to Father,' Jenny said. 'I'm very happy with you, but he's probably very sad. He doesn't know if I am alive or dead.'

◆

The summer ended and the winter passed. Early one morning, Fritz went out in his canoe. He was looking for a nice big fish for our lunch. Then, suddenly, we saw him turn round and come back.

'Quick! Quick!' he cried. 'There's a ship!'

We ran up to the top of a hill with our guns.

'BANG!' There was an answering shot from far away.

We waited, then used the gun again, and the answer came, louder and nearer. Then we saw a boat coming towards the beach. We ran down to meet it. An officer stepped out.

'I am Officer Littleton,' he said, 'of the *Unicorn*. Is Miss Jenny Montrose here? Some of the sailors from her ship, the *Dorcas*, told me to try these islands, because the ship was lost near here.'

'Yes,' I said, 'Miss Jenny Montrose is here, and she's safe.'

He looked at me and my family, and at Jenny in sailors' clothes.

'But . . .' he said.

I told him my name. 'And this is my wife . . . my sons Fritz . . . Ernest . . . Jack . . . Franz . . . and this,' I said, 'is Jenny, our Jenny.'

Chapter 17   The End

I am writing this chapter with a sad heart.

The *Unicorn*'s boat is waiting to take this story of our life here to England. There, perhaps, it will become a book. Other people will learn about our beautiful island, and perhaps some will want to join us in this quiet, simple, happy life.

I asked my children, 'Do you want to go back to Europe, boys, or to stay here?'

Ernest said, 'I want to stay and learn more about the plants, but the officer must send me books.'

Jack and Franz were too small to go.

I turned to Fritz. 'And you, Fritz? Do you want to go back to Europe?'

He took Jenny's hand in his. 'Yes,' he said, 'we want to go now, but we'll come back.'

Officer Littleton left us some things, and we gave him our pearls.

'I'll send you more from Europe,' he promised. 'I'll sell the pearls for you to pay for them and for Fritz's school.'

I must stop. The boat is waiting.

Goodbye, my boy. Goodbye, Jenny. Until we meet again!

ACTIVITIES

Chapters 1–3

Before you read

1 Like Robinson Crusoe, the Swiss Family Robinson are lost on a small island in the middle of the ocean. Imagine this happens to you. How will you feel? What will you do?

2 Look at the Word List at the back of the book. Read through the meanings. Find two things to help you:

   a cross a river.

   b grow some vegetables.

   c pull heavy things across snow or sand.

While you read

3 How many people are in the Swiss Family Robinson (✓)?

   4 .....   5 .....   6 .....

4 Which of these things do they take from the ship on their first visit to the island (✓)?

   a guns and gunpowder .....   **f** food   .....

   b a box of tools   .....   **g** dogs   .....

   c a donkey   .....   **h** goats   .....

   d a pig   .....   **i** sheep   .....

   e chickens   .....   **j** coconuts .....

5 When they get to the island, what do they do first? Number these sentences, 1–8.

   a Add a baby monkey to their family.   .....

   b Catch a large shellfish.   .....

   c Eat a meal.   .....

   d Find sugar plants.   .....

   e Look for other people on the island.   .....

   f Make a fire.   .....

   g Make a tent.   .....

   h Make pots and plates from gourds.   .....

After you read

6 Your ship has hit rocks. You have to leave quickly and swim to an island. You can only take three things. What will you take? What do other students take?

7 Work in pairs. You are two of the Swiss Family Robinson boys. It is the first night on the island. It is dark and you are lying on beds of dry grass. There is a gun between you. How do you feel? Have a conversation.

Chapters 4–5

Before you read

8 Most of the animals are still on the ship. The family's boat is small. How will they get the animals to the island? Is it a good idea to keep so many animals? Why (not)? Discuss your ideas with other students.

While you read

9 Which is the right word?

  a The animals on the ship are *hungry / healthy*.

  b A *light / piece of cloth* shows the mother that the father and Fritz are safe on the ship.

  c Fritz and his father spend *one night / two nights* on the ship.

  d The barrels help the animals *to swim / when they are tired of swimming*.

  e Fritz thinks *the goats / the pig* will be the most useful.

10 Who or what:

  a says they must build a tree house? ....

  b says they can find wood on the beach? ....

  c refuses to carry anything? ....

  d can't catch the chickens? ....

  and ....

  e carries the chickens to the new home? ....

  f tries the bridge first? ....

11 Discuss these questions.

 a What dangers will there be for the family on the island, do you think? Write a list.

 b The mother does all the cooking in this family. Who does the cooking in your family?

Chapters 6–8

Before you read

12 Have you ever been in a tree house? Who built it? How will the family build a tree house? How will they get up and down to the house after it is built? Talk to other students.

While you read

13 Complete each sentence with one of these words.

 shoot make put cut pull tie

 To make a rope ladder:

 a .... bamboo into short pieces.

 b .... two long pieces of rope on the ground.

 c .... bamboo pieces across the rope.

 To hang up a rope ladder:

 d .... a bow and arrows with sticks, bamboo and nails.

 e Tie a thin rope to an arrow and .... it over the tree branch.

 f Tie the ladder to the thin rope and .... it over the branch.

14 Circle the wrong word. Write the correct word.

 a They make the roof of the Tree House from bamboo. ....

 b They find a ladder in Ernest's box of tools. ....

 c The mother isn't afraid of the ladder but she climbs up it. ....

 d The father says they can shoot small animals with their guns. ....

 e Ernest and Jack shoot two large birds. ....

 f They decide to eat the potatoes that they find in a bag. ....

15 Have you ever looked for things on a beach? What did you find? Talk to another student about this.

16 You are going to be alone on an island for six months. You can take one book, one CD and have one favourite meal. What will you choose? What do other students choose?

Chapters 9–11

Before you read

17 Fritz and his father go back to the ship again in Chapter 10. What will they bring back this time, do you think?

While you read

18 Find the right end to these sentences.

a They use the sledge to . . .	have babies in the forest.
b The chickens . . .	make bread.
c The donkey won't be able to . . .	move bamboo to the Tree
d They use a line to . . .	House.
e They use sweet potatoes to . . .	produce their first eggs.
f The pig is going to . . .	carry heavy things.
g They use the river to . . .	pull the plough.
	catch a fish on the way back.

After you read

19 Answer these questions.

    a Why do the animals need huts?

    b Why do the chickens need a safe place?

    c Why does the writer think they can only make one more journey to the ship?

    d What are the most useful things they find on their second journey?

    e Why can't the big fish pull them out to sea?

    f How does the fish taste?

    g Why do they need a wall round the garden?

    h Why will the pig need a big hut?

20 Work in pairs. Imagine you have been on the island for a long time. Think of three ways to get off the island. Tell your ideas to other pairs. Who has the best ideas?

Chapters 12–13

Before you read

21 Discuss these questions and make notes.

    a What will they find when they go up river?

    b What problems will the family have in the winter?

While you read

22 Are these sentences right (✓) or wrong (✗)?

    a Nine people and animals go on a journey up the river.   .....

    b The two dogs find some wild horses.   .....

    c The dogs kill one of the buffaloes.   .....

    d The buffaloes can pull the plough in the garden.   .....

    e The pig comes back with little pigs but the donkey comes back alone.   .....

    f The animals will eat dry grass in the winter.   .....

23 Complete each sentence with one word.

    a The sea is coming up the beach towards their boat, so they pull it .... up.

    b The sailor's clothes are wet and .... , so they wash them in the river.

    c They need food near the house, so they have .... of salt meat and buffalo meat.

    d The Tree House is high, so the .... gets under the sailcloth roof.

    e They are wet and cold in the Tree House, so they build a .... room at the foot of the tree.

    f There isn't enough .... for the animals, so they kill four of the young dogs.

After you read

24 The stormy sea breaks up the ship. How do the boys feel when the ship is gone, do you think?

56

Chapters 14–15

Before you read

25 Discuss these questions. How will the family feel when the storms
end and the sun shines again? Will they try to leave the island? If
not, what will they do before next winter?

While you read

26 Choose the best words to complete each sentence.

    a The mother doesn't want to spend next winter

       in the Tree House.   in a cave.

    b The father finds a cave

       in the side of a hill.   near a river.

    c They can't go into Jack's cave because

       they can't see.   the air is bad.

    d To get the bad air out of the cave, they use

       burning grass.   gunpowder.

    e In the cave, they find lots of

       wood.   salt.

    f When the cave is ready, the mother is very

       pleased with it.   unhappy about it.

27 Which son:

    a is small and quiet and not as lazy as he was?   ....

    b is closer to his father?   ....

    c is strong and tall and makes a canoe?   ....

    d is closer to his mother?   ....

After you read

28 The mother and father are very good at making things and growing
things. What skills do you have that are useful for a life like this?
Tell the class.

29 Work with another student. Have this conversation.

    Student A: You are the father. You think life on the island is good
                 for the children. Tell your wife why.

    Student B: You are the mother. You are worried about the
                 children. What about school and friends? Discuss
                 your worries with your husband.

Chapters 16–17

Before you read

30 The next chapter is called 'Jenny'. What will Fritz find when he goes on an adventure with his canoe, do you think?

While you read

31 What two things does Fritz find at the beginning of his journey?
Some large .... and a .... written in blood.

32 Complete Jenny's story with these words.

built eats has been is living is waiting made was lost

Jenny .... alone on a small island. She .... there for a year. Her ship .... in a storm a year ago. She .... a hut from branches. She .... shellfish, coconuts and small fish. She .... a fishing line from her hair. She .... for Fritz.

33 Write one-word answers to these questions.

   a What can Jenny do better than the boys?   ....

   b What does she know more about than
     the boys?   ....

   c How do they tell the ship that they are
     on the island? What do they use?   ....

   d What is the ship called?   the ....

   e What was Jenny's ship called?   the ....

After you read

34 Are you surprised by the ending? What will happen to the family in the future, do you think?

Writing

35 Fritz and Jenny left the island a year ago. You are Fritz's mother. Write to Fritz and tell him about your life now. Do you still want to stay? Do you want to go?

36 You are Fritz. You left the island with Jenny a year ago. Write to your mother and father. Tell them what has happened since then.

37 Write a description of the island.

38 Imagine this is your second year alone on the island. You find an old glass bottle on the beach one day. Write a message to put in the bottle and send out to the world.

39 Compare your life with the life of the Swiss Family Robinson. How different is it? Is it similar in any way?

40 You work for a newspaper in a big city. You are on a ship that visits the island. You ask the boys about life on the island. Write your questions and their answers.

41 You are a reporter. You have been on the island with the family and now you are back in the city. Write a report about the family for your newspaper.

42 You are writing a travel guide to the islands in this area. Write about the Swiss Family Robinson's island for the guide. Put in information from your imagination if you don't have it.

43 You find yourself on a small island after a plane crash. You have been there for six months when you suddenly meet another person. What will you say? Write your first conversation.

44 You get back to a city after a year alone on an island. Describe what you do on your first day.

Answers for the Activities in this book are available from the Pearson English Readers website. A free Activity Worksheet is also available from the website. Activity worksheets are part of the Pearson English Readers Teacher Support Programme, which also includes Progress tests and Graded Reader Guidelines. For more information, please visit: www.pearsonenglishreaders.com

WORD LIST

arrow (n) a thin, straight stick with a point at one end that is shot at people or animals

bamboo (n) a tall plant that is used for light furniture

bark (n) the outside part of a tree

barrel (n) a large wooden thing that beer, for example, is kept in

bow (n) the piece of equipment that you shoot arrows from

branch (n) one of the parts of a tree that grow up and out from it

canoe (n) a long, light, narrow boat

cave (n) a large natural hole in the side of a hill or under the ground

coconut (n) a large, round, hard brown fruit with a soft white centre that grows on trees in hot countries

corn (n) something that is grown for use in food like bread

gourd (n) a large fruit with a hard outside that people sometimes keep things in

gunpowder (n) something that people put in guns in the past. When you light it, it can destroy buildings and walls of rock.

nail (n/v) a thin, pointed piece of metal with one flat end that can, for example, join two pieces of wood

paddle (n) a short stick with a wide, flat end used for moving a small boat through the water

pearl (n) a small, round, expensive white thing that comes from a sea animal. Women wear pearls around their necks.

plough (n) a piece of farm equipment that turns the earth

rope (n) something strong and thick that you use for tying things

seed (n) a small, hard thing that a new plant can grow from

shell (n) the hard outside part that covers some sea animals

sledge (n) a vehicle that you can pull. In snow, dogs sometimes pull a sledge while people sit on it.

Better learning
comes from fun.

Pearson English **Readers**

There are plenty of Pearson English Readers to choose from
- world classics, film and television adaptations, short stories, thrillers,
modern-day crime and adventure, biographies, American classics,
non-fiction, plays ... and more to come.

For a complete list of all Pearson English Readers titles, please contact
your local Pearson Education office or visit the website.

pearsonenglishreaders.com

Notes:

Notes:

_____

_____

_____

_____

_____

_____

_____

_____

_____

_____

_____

_____

_____

_____

_____

_____

LONGMAN
Dictionaries

Express yourself with confidence

Longman has led the way in ELT dictionaries since 1935. We constantly talk to students and teachers around the world to find out what they need from a learners' dictionary.

Why choose a Longman dictionary?

EASY TO UNDERSTAND

Longman invented the Defining Vocabulary - 2000 of the most common words which are used to write the definitions in our dictionaries. So Longman definitions are always clear and easy to understand.

REAL, NATURAL ENGLISH

All Longman dictionaries contain natural examples taken from real-life that help explain the meaning of a word and show you how to use it in context.

AVOID COMMON MISTAKES

Longman dictionaries are written specially for learners, and we make sure that you get all the help you need to avoid common mistakes. We analyse typical learners' mistakes and include notes on how to avoid them.

DIGITAL INNOVATION

Longman dictionaries are also available online at:
www.longmandictionaries.com or **www.longmandictionariesusa.com**

These are premier dictionary websites that allow you to access the best of Longman Learners' dictionaries, whatever you do, wherever you are. They offer a wealth of additional resources for teachers and students in the Teacher's Corner and the Study Centre.